CW00968175

to my darling Henry
with love from your
biggest sister, Lotte
XXX

Happy 3rd
Birthday!

# ZEN TAILS™

## UP AND DOWN

WRITTEN BY PETER WHITFIELD

ILLUSTRATED BY NANCY BEVINGTON

NEW FRONTIER PUBLISHING

Monkey was very bored.

"Bored, bored, bored!" Monkey cried.
"There is absolutely, positively, definitely,
nothing whatsoever to do!"

Monkey had been bored for days. "I will ask Shri Shelly the tortoise to give me something to do," he muttered, "and if she doesn't give me anything to do I will bash her house down."

Bashing Shri Shelly's house down would be something to do.

Monkey ran over to Shri Shelly who was sitting alone on a hill overlooking a river. Shelly smiled and waved to Monkey as he approached.

"Hello Monkey, how are you today?" Shelly asked.

"I'm bored," Monkey moaned. "Please Shelly, give me something to do." Shelly shook her head slightly, as there was nothing that needed to be done.

"Give me something to do," demanded Monkey. "If you don't I will bash your house down."

"My house is my shell," said Shelly.

"Well I will smash up your shell!" shrieked Monkey, annoyed.

S helly thought for a moment.

"Lets have some lemonade."

Even that sounded boring to Monkey, but he
watched as Shelly disappeared inside her shell and
pulled out two glasses of lemonade, a table and
chairs. Shelly's house was really quite amazing.

Monkey guzzled the lemonade in one gulp.

"Give me something else to do," he demanded.

"Why don't you take the glasses down to the river and wash them up?" suggested Shelly.

Monkey grabbed the glasses and rushed down to the river. But he was so quick that it wasn't a minute before he was back, demanding something else to keep him occupied.

Shelly suddenly had a great idea.

"Just a moment!" she said as she disappeared into her shell and pulled out an enormous ladder. It was at least thirty times longer than Shelly's house, but Monkey was too bored to notice how amazing this was.

"Monkey, I want you to climb to the top of this ladder. When you reach the top I want you to climb back down. When you reach the bottom you are to climb back up again. Repeat this until I come and give you something else to do."

Monkey took the ladder happily and planted it firmly into the ground.

He ran up the ladder.

He ran down the ladder.

He ran up,

Then down.

# UP

# DOWN

# UP

# DOWN

Hundreds of times Monkey scaled the ladder.

And hundreds of times he ran back down.

A few hours later Shelly came back to check on Monkey.

"Why aren't you climbing the ladder?" Shelly asked when she found Monkey sitting breathlessly at the bottom.

"I got tired and couldn't climb anymore," Monkey replied.

"So do you feel better now?" Shelly asked.

M onkey thought about it for a moment.

"No, I just ran up and down the ladder," he replied, surprised. "I didn't play any games, or have tea with my friend Grizzel. I didn't even go coconut hunting, which is my favourite thing in the whole world."

Shelly smiled at Monkey, took down the ladder and put it back inside her incredible shell.

"It's a shame you were too bored to think of anything fun to do, Monkey," Shelly said wisely. "And now that you have thought of lots of things, you're too tired to do them!"

Monkey frowned. He had wasted his entire day and had nothing to show for it at all.
"Maybe," Shelly said kindly, "you won't be too tired tomorrow to do some fun things."

Monkey looked up at Shelly happily.
"Or too bored!" he replied, and he scurried off planning all the exciting things he would do tomorrow.

# Zen

A holy man was approached by a powerful giant who
said that he would do the man's work for him on the
condition that he must be kept busy; if the giant ran out of work
he would devour the man. The man thought there was plenty to do,
so the giant could be kept busy like any ordinary being, but the giant
was very quick in completing the tasks and returning for more orders,
and very soon he finished all the work the man could think of.
Now the man had an idea, and asked the giant to cut a bamboo pole
and bring it to him and fix it in the courtyard. When the giant had
fixed it firmly there, the man said, "Unless I ask you to come and
do a special job, your general job is to go up and down this
pole." Going continually up and down the pole exhausted
the giant very quickly, who then settled down at the
bottom of the pole to wait for the next
order from the holy man.

# Tail

The restless mind is an horrendous master.

The calm mind is a wonderful servant.

If you think you are bored or dissatisfied with life, then stop, as Monkey finally did, and look again. You will find that there are plenty of interesting, useful and wonderful things to occupy your time and you can enjoy life.

New Frontier Publishing
ABN 25 192 683 466
6 Merle Street,
Epping, NSW , 2121, AUSTRALIA
www.newfrontier.com.au

First published in Australia in 2004

Text copyright © 2004 Peter Whitfield
Illustrations copyright © 2004 Nancy Bevington

This book is copyright. Apart from any fair dealing for the purposes of
private study, research, criticism or review, as permitted by the Copyright
Act 1968, no part may be reproduced by any process without written
permission. Inquiries should be addressed to the publishers.

All rights reserved.

National Library of Australia Cataloguing-in-Publication data:
Whitfield, Peter, 1962-.
Zen tails: Up and down

ISBN 0 9750907 3 9

I. Zen - Juvenile fiction. I. Bevington, Nancy. II. Title.
III. Title : Up and Down (Series : Zen Tails no. 2).

Designed by Nancy Bevington
Edited by Gabiann Marin & Christina Karaviotis

Printed in Hong Kong